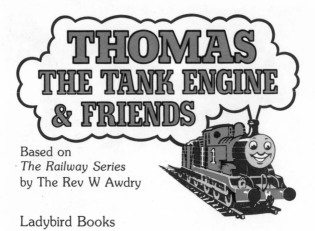

THOMAS THE TANK ENGINE & FRIENDS

Based on
The Railway Series
by The Rev W Awdry

Ladybird Books

Acknowledgment
Photographic stills by Kenny McArthur of Clearwater Features for Britt Allcroft Ltd.

British Library Cataloguing in Publication Data
Awdry, W.
   Thomas & Bertie; Thomas down the mine.—
   (Thomas the tank engine & friends)
   I. Title   II. Awdry, W. Thomas down the mine
   III. McArthur, Kenny   IV. Series
   823′.914[J]   PZ7
   ISBN 0-7214-0893-1

THOMAS AND BERTIE

Thomas and Bertie

One day Thomas was waiting at the junction when a bus came into the yard.

"Hullo!" said Thomas. "Who are you?"

"I'm Bertie," said the bus. "Who are you?"

"I'm Thomas. I run this branch line."

Bertie laughed. "Ah – I remember now!" he said. "You were stuck in the snow. I had to take your passengers, then Terence the tractor had to pull you out! I've come to help you with your passengers today."

"Help *me*?" said Thomas, crossly.
"I can go faster than you," he said, going
bluer than ever and letting off steam.

"You can't," said Bertie.

"I can," huffed Thomas.

"I'll race you!" said Bertie.

Their drivers agreed to the race. The Station Master shouted, "Are you ready? GO!" – and they were off!

It always took Thomas a little while to build up speed so Bertie quickly drew in front.

Thomas was running well but he did not hurry. "Why don't you go fast? Why don't you go fast?" called Annie and Clarabel, who were running along behind.

"Wait and see. Wait and see," hissed Thomas.

"He's a long way ahead, a long way ahead," they cried, anxiously.

But Thomas didn't mind; he had
remembered the level crossing.

There was Bertie fuming at the crossing
gates while they sailed gaily through.

"Goodbye, Bertie!" called Thomas.

After that the road left the railway and went through a village. They couldn't see Bertie any more.

Before long they had to stop at a station to let off passengers. "Peep, pip, peep! Quickly, please," called Thomas.

Everybody got out quickly. The guard blew his whistle and off they went again.

"Come along! Come along!" sang Thomas.

"We're coming along! We're coming along!" said Annie and Clarabel.

Thomas looked straight ahead and whistled in horror. There was Bertie crossing the bridge over the railway, tooting triumphantly on his horn!

"Oh, deary me! Oh, deary me!" groaned Thomas.

"Steady, Thomas," said Thomas's driver. "We'll beat Bertie yet."

Annie and Clarabel joined in. "We'll beat Bertie yet! We'll beat Bertie yet!" they sang.

"We'll do it! We'll do it!" puffed Thomas, bravely. "Oh bother, there's a station."

As Thomas stopped at the station he heard Bertie, tooting loudly.

"Goodbye, Thomas! You must be tired," called Bertie, as he raced by. "Sorry I can't stop; we *buses* have to work you know! Goodbye."

"Oh dear!" thought Thomas. "We've lost!" But he felt better after a drink. Then the signal dropped to show that the line was clear and they were off again.

As they rumbled over the bridge they saw Bertie waiting at the traffic lights. When the lights turned green, Bertie started with a roar and chased on after Thomas again.

17

Road and railway ran up the valley
side by side. By now Thomas had
reached his full speed. Bertie tried hard
but Thomas was too fast.

On and on they raced. Excited
passengers cheered and shouted across
the valley as Thomas whistled
triumphantly and plunged into the
tunnel, leaving Bertie toiling far behind.

"We've done it! We've done it!"
chanted Annie and Clarabel happily, as
they whooshed into the last station.

Everybody was there to give Thomas three cheers for winning the race. They all gave Bertie a big welcome too.

"Well done, Thomas!" said Bertie. "That was fun. But to beat you over that hill I should have had to grow wings and be an aeroplane!"

Now Thomas and Bertie keep each other very busy. Bertie finds people in the villages who want to go by train and takes them to Thomas, while Thomas brings people to the station for Bertie to take home.

Bertie and Thomas often talk about their race. But Bertie's passengers don't like being bounced like peas in a frying pan!

The Fat Controller has warned Thomas not to race at dangerous speeds. So although Thomas and Bertie would like to have another race, I don't think they ever will. Do you?

THOMAS
DOWN THE MINE

Thomas down the mine

One day Thomas was at the junction when Gordon shuffled in with some trucks.

"Poof!" said Thomas. "What a funny smell! Can you smell a smell?"

"I can't smell a smell," said Annie.

"It's a funny, musty sort of smell," said Thomas.

"No one noticed it until you did," grunted Gordon. "It must be yours!" Not long ago Gordon had fallen into a dirty ditch. He knew that Thomas was teasing him about it.

"Annie and Clarabel, do you know what *I* think it is?" said Thomas. "It's ditchwater!" Gordon didn't have time to answer as Thomas was soon coupled to Annie and Clarabel and then he puffed quickly away.

Annie and Clarabel could hardly believe their ears. "He's *dreadfully* rude, I feel quite ashamed, I feel *quite* ashamed, he's dreadfully rude!" they twittered to each other.

They had great respect for Gordon, the big engine. "You mustn't be rude, you make us ashamed," they kept telling Thomas. But Thomas didn't care a bit.

"That was funny, that was funny," he chuckled, feeling very pleased with himself.

Thomas left the coaches at the station and went off to a mine for some trucks.

Long ago, miners digging for lead had made tunnels under the ground. The tunnel roofs were strong enough to hold trucks, but they could not take the weight of the heavy engines.

A large notice said: "DANGER
ENGINES MUST NOT PASS THIS POINT"

Thomas had been warned but he
didn't care. He had often tried to pass
the sign before but had never succeeded.
He knew the rules; he had to push

empty trucks into one siding and wait to collect full ones from another.

This morning he laughed as he puffed along. He had made a plan. "Silly old board!" he said to himself, getting nearer and nearer to the danger sign.

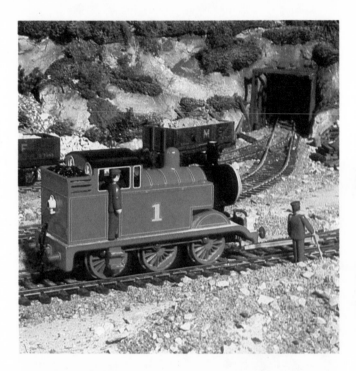

The driver stopped him and the fireman went to turn the points. "Now for my plan," said Thomas and he bumped the trucks fiercely, jerking the driver off the footplate!

"Hurrah!" said Thomas, as he followed the trucks into a siding.

"Come back!" called his driver. But it was too late.

"Stupid old board!" said Thomas, as he ran past it. "There's no danger! There's no danger!"

"Look out!" cried the driver. The fireman clambered into the cab and tried Thomas's brakes.

There was a rumbling noise and the rails quivered. The fireman jumped clear. Then the rails sagged and broke.

"Fire and smoke!" said Thomas. "I'm sunk!" – and he was! Thomas could just see out of the hole but he couldn't move. "Oh dear!" he said. "I *am* a silly engine."

"And a very naughty one, too," said the Fat Controller, who had just arrived. "I saw you."

"Please get me out. I won't be naughty again," said Thomas.

"I'm not sure," said the Fat Controller. "We can't lift you out with a crane because the ground is not firm enough. Hmm...let me see...I wonder if Gordon could pull you out."

"Yes, sir," said Thomas, nervously. He didn't want to see Gordon just yet.

When Gordon heard about Thomas he laughed very loudly. "Down a mine is he? Ho! Ho! Ho! What a joke! What a joke!" he chortled, puffing quickly to the rescue.

"Poop! Poop! Little Thomas," Gordon whistled. "We'll have you out in a couple of puffs. Poop! Poop! Poop!"

The men fastened strong cables between Gordon and Thomas.

"Are you ready? HEAVE!" called the Fat Controller.

But they didn't pull Thomas out in two puffs. It was a lot harder than they had

all thought. Gordon worked hard but it took a long time to finally pull Thomas out of the hole.

"I'm sorry I was cheeky," said Thomas.

"That's all right, Thomas," said Gordon. "You made me laugh!" Thomas was very pleased that Gordon was not angry with him any more.

Thomas's fire had gone out so he needed a pull back to the station. "Can we go together?" asked Thomas.

"Of course we can," said Gordon. "I'll pull you back."

"Thank you very much," said Thomas. And buffer to buffer the two friends puffed home.